Grandma, Felix, and Mustapha Biscuit

Victor G Ambrus

Oxford University Press

Oxford University Press, Walton Street, Oxford OX2 6DP

Oxford New York Toronto
Delhi Bombay Calcutta Madras Karachi
Petaling Jaya Singapore Hong Kong Tokyo
Nairobi Dar es Salaam Cap Town
Melbourne Auckland

and associated companies in
Berlin Ibadan

Oxford is a trade mark of Oxford University Press

ISBN 0 19 279789 1
Printed in Hong Kong

Grandma, Felix the cat, and Long John Silver the parrot
all lived happily together in a little old house.

One day Grandma came home carrying a small box with holes on the top and a new cage.

Out of the box and into the cage went the plumpest,
tastiest-looking little thing that Felix had ever seen.
Grandma told Felix and Long John that he was a hamster
and that his name was Mustapha Biscuit.
Every time he saw a biscuit he said to himself, 'I must have
a biscuit!'

That night Felix dreamed of hamsters on toast, hamsters with tomato sauce, and grilled hamsters with gravy and vegetables.

In the morning Grandma put on her best hat to go out shopping and told Long John and Felix to behave themselves.

But, as soon as she left, Felix got hold of a safety-pin and started to pick the lock on Mustapha's cage.
He was so busy that he didn't notice Mustapha Biscuit admiring his bushy tail.
To make the cage really comfortable Mustapha wanted to build a cosy sleeping nest.
Felix's tail would give him just the material he needed!

Happily Mustapha began to pluck the lovely hairs out of
Felix's tail.
He was surprised that he needed so many, but Felix didn't
seem to mind, so he took more and more of them.

By the time Grandma came home with her groceries,
Mustapha Biscuit had a fine soft nest and Felix had a
very bald tail.
Grandma had a good laugh and said
'Serves you right, you greedy old cat!
That will teach you to go after hamsters.'

Still, when Grandma saw how Felix shivered with cold
because of his bald tail, she took pity on him.
As quick as could be, she knitted him a brightly coloured
tail sweater that fitted him perfectly.

Now Felix had a nice warm tail again.
But every time he went out all the alley cats howled with
laughter.
Angrily Felix swore a terrible revenge against Mustapha.
He would make him pay for his multicoloured tail!

The day came when Grandma had to go out on another long shopping trip.
Once again she put on her best hat and told the animals to behave themselves.

But, as soon as she left, Felix took a chocolate-covered
biscuit with pink sugar sprinkles from the dish on the table.

He wanted Mustapha out of his cage, and it would
make a tasty bait.
Mustapha could not believe his luck when the biscuit
suddenly appeared.
'I must have a biscuit,' he said to himself.

With all his strength, he pulled apart two bars in his cage.
But just as he was about to get hold of that lovely biscuit . . .

. . . Felix pounced!

YA-iAOOOOw....

But Mustapha bit him on his paw and jumped for
Long John's cage.

'Run for your lives, mates!' shouted Long John, and he flew
out of the open door.

Long John escaped just in time.
As Mustapha jumped into the cage Felix leaped in after
him . . . and got stuck.
The harder he struggled, the more tightly he wedged
himself in.

Mustapha went back to his cage, and Long John moved
in with him.
Peacefully they shared the sunflower seeds with each other.

When Grandma came back and found Felix in the parrot's
cage, she laughed herself silly.
'Serves you right, you greedy thing,' she cried.

He He He...

Grandma had to take Felix to the vet to get him out of
the cage.
Once again all the alley cats howled with laughter when
they saw Felix trapped inside a parrot's cage with his
multicoloured tail dangling between the bars.

But the worst was yet to come.
Felix had bald places rubbed off around his wrists and
ankles, and he had to wear special cuffs that Grandma
knitted for him.
Grandma only laughed and told Felix that his greed
would be the end of him.
But Felix didn't hear.
He was too busy plotting another terrible revenge. . . .